TREES MAKE PERFECT PETS

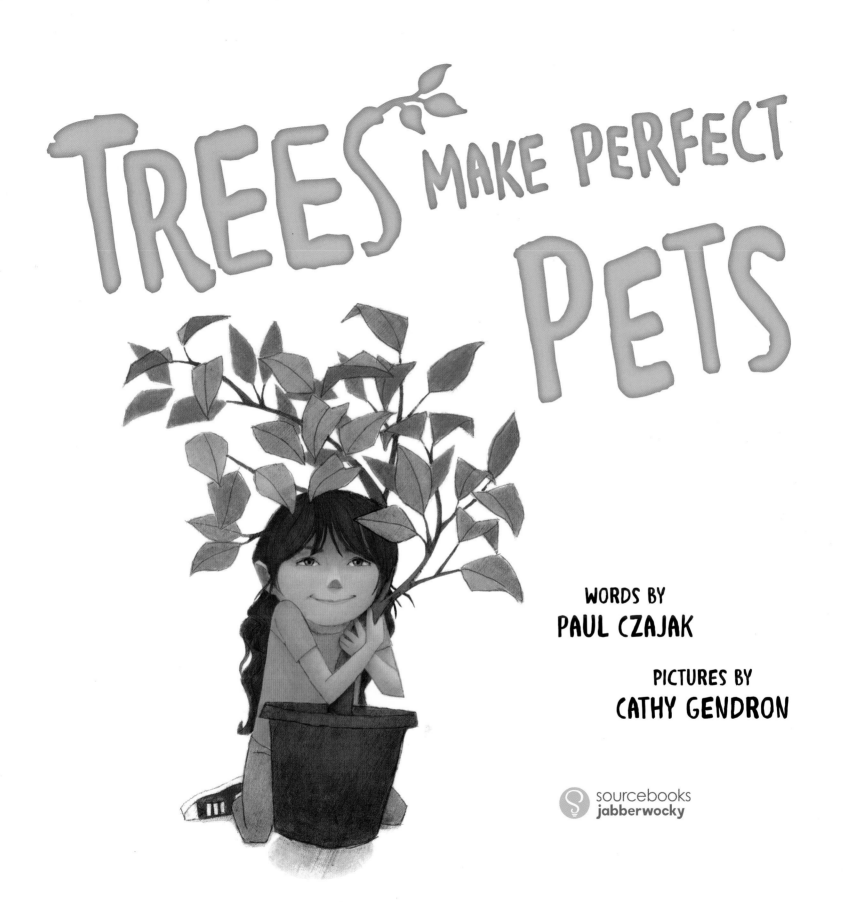

WORDS BY
PAUL CZAJAK

PICTURES BY
CATHY GENDRON

sourcebooks
jabberwocky

TO ABIGAIL. YES, WE'LL GET A DOGWOOD, BUT YOU HAVE TO NAME IT.
—PC

TO GREEN THUMBS EVERYWHERE.
—CG

Text © 2020 by Paul Czajak
Illustrations © 2020 Cathy Gendron
Cover and internal design © 2020 by Sourcebooks

The art was first sketched in pencil and then painted on textured gesso with casein and oil glazes.

Published by Sourcebooks Jabberwocky, an imprint of Sourcebooks Kids
P.O. Box 4410, Naperville, Illinois 60567-4410
(630) 961-3900
sourcebookskids.com

Library of Congress Cataloging-in-Publication data is on file with the publisher.

Source of Production: Leo Paper, Heshan City, Guangdong Province, China
Date of Production: November 2019
Run Number: 5016554

Printed and bound in China.
LEO 10 9 8 7 6 5 4 3 2 1

Birthdays are the best days for wishes and on
this birthday Abigail wished for a pet.

Her brother wanted a dog.
    "They're man's best friend."

Her father suggested a hamster.
    "They're so fluffy!"

Her mom thought a bird would be
nice. "They make beautiful music."

Abigail had another idea.

"I want a tree."

"A WHAT?" they all gasped.

"A tree. They're the greatest pets in the world."

"But a tree isn't a pet," her mom argued.

"Of course it is." Abigail said. "It's quiet. Easy to take care of. And can you name another pet that actually helps you breathe?"

Her family was stumped.

Abigail ran to the car.
"Let's go adopt a tree!"

Abigail searched the nursery and found her tree.
"He looks friendly."

"It's a tree. They're all friendly," her brother said.

"I'll name you Fido. You and I are going to be best friends."

Abigail and Fido were
always together.

"Shouldn't trees sleep outside?" her father asked.

"Fido would be lonely without me."

Abigail took good care of Fido. She watered him.
Sang to him. They loved going on long walks.

"What are you doing?" her neighbor asked.

"I'm taking Fido for a walk."

"That's a tree. Trees don't go for walks."

"This one does. He's my pet."

"A tree is not a good pet.
Cats are much better.
Oprah Whiskers
can cuddle."

"Fido loves a good hug."

"Oprah Whiskers can do tricks."

"Stay, Fido. Good boy."

"Oprah Whiskers keeps
me warm at night."

"Fido keeps me cool
during the day."

"Hmm, have it your way," her neighbor said.
"But a tree isn't a real pet."

Abigail took Fido to the dog park. She knew it was important for pets to socialize, but some didn't agree.

"I'm sorry, this park is for dogs."

"Fido is a *dog*wood."

"That doesn't count."

"He's very friendly. His bark is worse than his bite."

"Sorry, actual pets only."

Abigail didn't care what
other people thought of Fido.

She didn't mind
that Fido couldn't
go where other pets
could.

She didn't mind that Fido was
only good at fetching kites, and
didn't like to give them back.

She didn't mind that he
sometimes had accidents.

None of that mattered,
because Fido was her pet.

But like all pets, Fido grew.

Walks became more difficult.

Fido was a tight fit in her room at night.

And the breakfast table became crowded.

"There are leaves in my cereal again."

"Honey, Fido is too big to live in the house. He needs a permanent home," her mom said.

"But Fido is my friend. Where would he live?"

"Outside. A tree belongs in the ground," her father explained.

Abigail's heart
broke. Fido had grown
too big for the house.

Keeping him
inside was not
fair to him.

She found a sunny spot
in the yard, and dug him
a new home, but Abigail
wasn't ready to let go.

Worried that Fido felt scared and alone, Abigail kept him company under the stars.

When morning came, Abigail woke up to birds singing.

"Mom, Dad, come quick!"

Her family rushed outside to see what the commotion was.

"Fido made new friends!"

"I guess a tree can be man's best friend," her brother said.

Abigail hugged Fido.
"A tree is **everyone's** best friend."

Do you love trees just like Abigail? Well, you can help trees in your community grow big and strong like Fido! Trees make great friends, and they also make the world a better place for everyone. But, trees need help. Lots of trees get cut down and not enough get planted!

Ask your parents or teacher to go to the following websites and see how you can help these tree-friendly foundations make sure there are enough trees for everyone to have a friend:

· treesforachange.com/collections/green-fundraising

· earthday.org/campaigns/reforestation

· arborday.org/programs

· nationalforests.org/get-involved/tree-planting-programs